Humpty Dumpty
and other rhymes

templar publishing

To Monika and Luka

A TEMPLAR BOOK

Picture book edition first published in the UK in 2005 by Templar Publishing
This padded edition published in 2014 by Templar Publishing,
an imprint of The Templar Company Limited,
Deepdene Lodge, Deepdene Avenue, Dorking, Surrey, RH5 4AT, UK
www.templarco.co.uk

Copyright © 1999, 2002, 2005 by The Templar Company Limited

1 3 5 7 9 10 8 6 4 2

All rights reserved

ISBN 978-1-84877-181-9

Designed by janie louise hunt and Jonathan Lambert
Edited by Dug Steer and Sue Harris

Printed in China

Contents

Hey diddle diddle,
The cat and the fiddle,
The cow jumped over the moon;
The little dog laughed
To see such fun,
And the dish ran away
with the spoon.

Incy Wincy spider
climbed up the spout,[1]
Down came the raindrops[2]
and washed poor Incy out.[3]

Out came the sunshine
and dried up all the rain,[4]
So Incy Wincy spider
climbed up the
spout again.[5]

Hickory, dickory dock,
The mouse ran up the clock.
The clock struck one,
The mouse ran down,
Hickory, dickory dock.

The wheels on the bus go round and round, round and round, round and round.

The wheels on the bus go round and round, all day long...1

The wipers on the bus go swish, **swish** **swish**...2

The riders on the bus go bumpety-bump bumpety-bump bumpety-bump...3

The babies on the bus go wah, **wah**, **WAH**...4

The mummies on the bus go **Shh! Shh! Shh!**...5

Repeat first verse.

The Queen of Hearts

She made some tarts
All on a summer's day;
The knave of hearts
He stole the tarts
And took them clean away.

Jack and Jill went up the hill

To fetch a pail of water;
Jack fell down and broke his crown
And Jill came tumbling after.

Five little ducks
went swimming one day[1]
Over the hills and far away,[2]
Mother Duck said,
"Quack, quack, quack, quack,"[3]
But only four little ducks came back.[4]

Four little ducks...
Three little ducks...
Two little ducks...
One little duck...

This little pig went to market,
This little pig stayed at home.
This little pig had roast beef,

This little pig had none. And this little pig cried, wee, wee, wee, all the way home.

Row, row
row your boat
gently down the stream.
Merrily, merrily, merrily, merrily,
life is but a dream.

Row, row, row your boat
gently down the stream.
If you see a crocodile,
don't forget to SCREAM!

There was a
crooked man,
and he walked a crooked mile,
He found a crooked sixpence
against a crooked stile;
He bought a crooked cat,
which caught a crooked mouse,
And they all lived together
in a little crooked house.

Baa, baa,
black sheep,
Have you any wool?
Yes, sir, yes, sir,
Three bags full;
One for the master,
And one for the dame,
And one for the little boy
Who lives down the lane.

The Grand Old
Duke of York,
He had ten thousand men;
He marched them up to
the top of the hill,
And he marched them
down again.

Rub-a-dub-dub,
Three men in a tub;
And who do you think they be?
The butcher, the baker,
the candlestick maker;
Turn 'em out, knaves all three!

Pat-a-cake, pat-a-cake,
baker's man,[1]
Bake me a cake as fast as you can;
Pat it and prick it,[2]
and mark it with B,[3]
Put it in the oven for
baby and me.[4]

Little Miss Muffet,
Sat on a tuffet,
Eating her curds and whey.
Along came a spider,
Who sat down beside her,
And frightened Miss Muffet away!

Wee Willie Winkie
runs through the town,
Upstairs and downstairs,
in his nightgown,
Rapping at the window,
crying at the lock,

"Are the children all in bed,
for now it's eight o'clock?"

The End